William Arnold Spicer

The Flag Replaced in Sumter

Volume 1

William Arnold Spicer

The Flag Replaced in Sumter
Volume 1

ISBN/EAN: 9783337090531

Printed in Europe, USA, Canada, Australia, Japan

Cover: Foto ©Andreas Hilbeck / pixelio.de

More available books at **www.hansebooks.com**

THE ATTACK ON FORT SUMTER IN APRIL, 1861.

THE

FLAG REPLACED ON SUMTER.

A PERSONAL NARRATIVE

BY

WILLIAM A. SPICER.

———•———

READ BEFORE THE

RHODE ISLAND SOLDIERS AND SAILORS HISTORICAL SOCIETY,

FEBRUARY, 1884.

———•———

PROVIDENCE:
PRINTED BY THE PROVIDENCE PRESS COMPANY.
1885.

THE FLAG REPLACED ON SUMTER.

"What's hallowed ground? 'Tis what gives birth
To sacred thoughts in souls of worth!
Peace! Independence! Truth!" — *Campbell.*

MMEDIATELY upon the election of Abraham Lincoln as President, in November, 1860, a predetermined plan of secession was entered upon by the leading public men of the South, on the plea that his election was dangerous to the interests of slavery. In February, 1861, seven of the slave States having united in the movement, an independent government was organized, under the name of the Southern Confederacy, and Jefferson Davis was inaugurated as President with great pomp, at Montgomery, Alabama; so that on the fourth of March, the day of Mr. Lincoln's inauguration at Washington, the flag of the United States was flying at only three points south of the Capital, viz: Fort Sumter, Fort Pickens, and Key West.

South Carolina naturally led the scheme of disunion, passing the ordinance of secession on the twentieth of December, 1860, and immediately proceeding to secure possession of the national property in the State, particularly the forts in Charleston harbor.

To prevent this, Major Robert Anderson, an able and loyal southern officer, commanding a small garrison of United States troops in Fort Moultrie, hastily removed, on the night of the 26th of December, to Fort Sumter, a much stronger but unfinished fortress in the middle of the harbor, hoping to maintain his position there till reinforced. But before this could be effected by President Lincoln, who had plainly advised Governor Pickens of his intention, a formal demand for the surrender of the fort was made by General Beauregard, commanding the rebel forces, which being promptly refused by Major Anderson, the order to reduce the fort was given by the Confederate government. On the morning of Friday, the twelfth of April, 1861, at half-past four, the first shot was fired upon Fort Sumter, which aroused and excited the nation, and begun the war of the Rebellion. For two days the assault continued, when after a most gallant defense by the little garrison of eighty men, Major Anderson was compelled to accept terms of evacuation. On Sunday afternoon, April 14th, he marched out of the fort with colors flying and drums beating, saluting the United States flag, as it was lowered, with fifty guns.

There was great rejoicing in Charleston. Thousands had assembled at the Battery, excited spectators of the scene. They exultingly beheld the banner of the Republic lowered, and the flags of South Carolina and the Southern Confederacy raised defiantly over the ramparts of Fort Sumter.

Governor Pickens, the bustling and blustering State executive, thus addressed the populace :

" We are now one of the Confederate States, and they have sent
us a brave and scientific officer, to whom the credit of this day's
triumph is due. We have defeated their twenty millions. We
have humbled the flag of the United States before the Palmetto
and Confederate, and so long as I have the honor to preside as your
chief magistrate, so help me God, there is no power on this earth
shall ever lower from that fortress those flags, unless they be lowered and trailed in a sea of blood. I can here say to you it is the
first time in the history of this country that the stars and stripes
have been humbled. That flag has never before been lowered
before any nation on this earth. But to-day it has been humbled,
and humbled before the glorious little State of South Carolina."

But Governor Pickens little dreamed that the dis-
charge of his guns upon the United States flag at
Fort Sumter would awaken such an outburst of
patriotism as immediately followed all over the
North, uniting the people of all classes in a determi-
nation to maintain the majesty of the Union, and
vindicate the honor of the flag. How little he fore-
saw the mighty sweep and terrible devastation of
the pitiless storm of civil war which now burst over
the land, and which never departed from the soil of
South Carolina till every rebel ensign was " lowered
and trailed in a sea of blood ; " till slavery, the cause
of the conflict, was forever abolished, and the power

of the United States firmly reëstablished on land and sea.

Four years had scarcely passed ere he heard the tramp of Sherman's army sweeping victoriously across the State, and beheld the once proud and haughty Charleston in possession of the Union legions. As he saw the starry flag again waving aloft in triumph, he hastened, with reluctant footsteps, to place himself once more under its protecting folds, thus renewing, in 1865, his oath of allegiance to the government whose authority he had defied in 1861 !

A few months later, at the State Convention at Columbia, assembled under the direction of the President of the United States, it is none other than our *reconstructed* friend, Ex-Governor Pickens, who rises amid the ashes of his once beautiful Capital, and offers the following ordinance :

"*Resolved*, We, the delegates of the people of the State of South Carolina, in general convention met, do ordain, that the ordinance [of secession] passed in convention on the twentieth of December, 1860, withdrawing this State from the Federal Union, be, and the same is, hereby repealed. The fortunes of war, together with the proclamation of the President of the United States, and the gener als in the field commanding, having decided that domestic slavery is abolished, that therefore, under the circumstances, we acquiesce in said proclamations, and do hereby ordain implicit obedience to the Constitution of the United States, and all laws made in pursuance thereof."

He had thus at last learned the truth of that ancient and profound maxim, that "he who would aspire to *govern*, should first learn *to obey!*"

General Sherman did not pause in his rapid march northward from Savannah, through the Carolinas, to make any demonstration against Charleston; he conquered it, in the words of General Robert Anderson, "by turning his *back* on it!" His military operations compelled the evacuation of the city, which was occupied by the Union troops on the eighteenth of February, 1865. Lieutenant-Colonel A. G. Bennett, of the Twenty-first United States colored troops, was the first to land with a small force, while some of the rebel mounted patrols still remained, applying the torch as they retreated. The Colonel at once addressed himself to the Mayor: "In the name of the United States government I demand a surrender of the city, of which you are the executive officer." The Mayor responded by immediately turning over the Cradle of Rebellion to its rightful owners. The Colonel then proceeded to the citadel with his colored troops, two companies of the Fifty-second Pennsylvania Regiment, and about thirty men of the Third Rhode Island Heavy Artillery, under Lieutenant-Colonel Ames, and proclaimed martial law. In his official report he says : "Every officer and soldier exerted himself to a most willing performance of every allotted duty, yet I do not deem it invidious for me to make special mention of Lieutenant John Hackett, Company M, Third Rhode Island Artillery, who volunteered to go alone to Fort Moultrie, and there raise the flag." This was a most perilous service, gallantly performed amid the danger of exploding rebel powder magazines.

It was the beginning of the end. President Lincoln, realizing that the fall of the Confederacy was near at hand, determined to celebrate the fourth anniversary of the surrender of Fort Sumter by replanting the old flag of 1861, with imposing ceremonies, upon the ruins of the fort, and the following order was accordingly issued :

GENERAL ORDERS, No. 50.

WAR DEPARTMENT, ADJUTANT GENERAL'S OFFICE,
WASHINGTON, March 27, 1865.

ORDERED: *First*, That at the hour of noon, on the 14th day of April, 1865, brevet Major-General Anderson will raise and plant upon the ruins of Fort Sumter, in Charleston harbor, the SAME United States flag which floated over the battlements of that fort during the rebel assault, and which was lowered and saluted by him, and the small force of his command, when the works were evacuated on the 14th of April, 1861.

Second, That the flag, when raised, be saluted by one hundred guns from Fort Sumter, and by a national salute from every fort and rebel battery that fired upon Fort Sumter.

Third, That suitable ceremonies be had upon the occasion, under the direction of Major-General William T. Sherman, whose military operations compelled the rebels to evacuate Charleston, or, in his absence, under the charge of Major-General Q. A. Gilmore, commanding the Department. Among the ceremonies will be the delivery of an address by the Rev. Henry Ward Beecher.

Fourth, That the naval forces at Charleston, and their commander on that station, be invited to participate in the ceremonies of the occasion.

Official.

By order of the President of the United States.

EDWIN M. STANTON, *Secretary of War.*

E. D. TOWNSHEND, *Assistant Adjutant-General.*

The steamer "Arago" was officially commissioned to carry to the fort those who were to take part in the exercises, and the gratifying announcement was afterwards received in Providence that a second steamer had been chartered, the "Oceanus," of our Neptune Propeller Line, to sail from New York for Charleston, on Monday, April 10th, at noon. Immediately, three Providence boys, two of us comrades in the Tenth Rhode Island Regiment, fired with the news just received of the fall of Richmond, made our plans for going to Charleston on the "Oceanus." We so well succeeded that on the morning of the tenth we made our appearance on the deck of the steamer, duly armed and equipped with the necessary papers and outfit.

There was great enthusiasm on board over the news from the seat of war, not only on account of the recent capture of Richmond and Petersburg, but because, during the night, the news had flashed over the wires of the surrender of Lee and the death of the Rebellion. We thus became the bearers of these glorious tidings to Fort Sumter and Charleston.

My reception of the news in New York is thus described in my diary : "Monday, April 10, Astor

2

House.   On coming down from my room this morning, my attention was arrested by the 'big letters'
at the head of the column of the morning paper, bearing the announcement of the surrender of General
Lee and his whole army.   It was pretty big news
to take *in*, and contain myself.   Passing into the
hotel parlors, I noticed that Broadway was gaily
decorated with flags (though the rain was descending in torrents), and there read in the *Herald*
the official documents from General Grant, upon
which I could hardly refrain from shouting three
cheers !   I believe I did give one !   While waiting
for breakfast I ventured, in the enthusiasm of the
moment, to seat myself at the piano, and was hard
at work on about the only patriotic tune I could
drum, viz : 'Tenting on the old camp ground,' when
a small boy came up with a message from some nice
looking young ladies at the opposite end of the
parlor, requesting 'The Star Spangled Banner,' in
honor of the glorious news.   Well, I didn't exactly
fall under the piano ; but briefly conveying regrets
at my inability to comply, I retired as gracefully as
possible."

Promptly at noon we waved our adieus from the deck of the "Oceanus" to the friends assembled on shore, and steamed slowly down the harbor. The weather was extremely rainy and foggy, and when hardly three hours out, we found ourselves aground on Sandy Hook bar. A pilot was signaled, who brought the report of a heavy storm outside, and after getting us safely off the sand-spit, he advised our "laying to" till morning. This was a great disappointment, as there was no time to lose, and some one impatiently asked, "Can't you take us out this afternoon, pilot?" "I reckon I can if you all say so," responded the old salt, "but you'd better lay *here*, to-night!" "Why so, pilot?" "You gentlemen want to go to Charleston, don't you?" "Why, yes, of course." "Wall, then, I tell you, you'd better lay *here* to-night, for it's goin' to be a werry nasty, dirty night outside." That settled the matter, and down went the big anchor of the "Oceanus."

Having eaten but sparingly during the day to avoid sea-sickness, and fully believing that we were firmly anchored for the night, I indulged in a hearty sup-

per, concluding, as my diary says, "with sardines
and oranges." I had occasion to feel very sorry
for this a few hours later.

A patriotic meeting was held in the cabin during
the evening. The music and addresses were very
enjoyable, till suddenly the sound of hurrying feet
was heard overhead, and the news was whispered
round that we were "weighing anchor." Soon we
began to feel the uncomfortable rolling of the steamer.
The orator who was then addressing the meeting,
and who had waxed eloquent with his subject, now
provoked considerable merriment by his ungraceful
and involuntary gestures, clutching desperately at a
chair, then taking a fresh hold of the table to steady
himself. It well illustrated Demosthenes' famous
rule for oratory, "Action! action! action!" But a
more serious impression quickly prevailed among
the audience, that it was high time to retire, and,
like Longfellow's Arabs, they began to "silently
steal away." The chairman of the meeting, Mayor
Wood, of Brooklyn, unmindful of his usual decorum,
upon an extra roll of the steamer went over the back

of his chair, and rolled ingloriously upon the floor. He acknowledged that he had never been so completely floored in his life.

There was another portly gentleman who, in attempting to navigate, was caught near the cabin door, just behind the knees, by a friendly chair, and as he was suddenly tilted back into it, remarked somewhat dryly, "I believe *I'll sit down!*" Going out on deck, I found that the storm had lifted, the lights of Sandy Hook were far astern, and we were fairly at sea. From this point of time on Monday evening, when we *lay* on deck, (things were getting too *unsteady* for landsmen to *stand,*) I omit, out of courtesy to ourselves, any further incidents of the voyage, and pass on to Thursday morning, which found us sitting on the forward deck, waiting and watching for the spires of Charleston. The weather was delightful. As we passed into the warmer southern climate, the sea became calmer and more transparent, schools of porpoises played about the steamer, and one enthusiastic individual insisted that he had seen a whale ! but he was set down by one of the disgruntled passengers as "only a pesky oil

speculator." The German band on board, or rather
the brief remnant of it, still kept up what at the distance of several yards sounded like very dismal
music! Presently some one suggested "lemons and
lump sugar," as the right remedy for any lingering
unpleasantness, and we drew lots as to who should
"go below," combat the smells of the cook-room, and
purchase them. The announcement that the chance
had fallen on my old friend and comrade of the
Tenth Rhode Island, William Vaughan, was greeted
with roars of laughter. But he got off very much
like another fellow described in Pickwick, who
spelled his name with a "double you" and a "wee,"
by liberally feeing some one else to go in his place.

About three o'clock in the afternoon came the joyful shout of "Land-ho!" which quickly filled the deck
of the "Oceanus" with a troop of smiling faces. All
gloom now gave way to sanguine expectation. We
could plainly distinguish the light-ship, bearing the
suggestive name, "Rattlesnake Shoals," and knew
we were at last off Charleston harbor. A pilot was
presently taken on board, who informed the captain
that we could not go over the bar till sunset. Some

one asked him, "Are the people over there in Charleston loyal now, pilot?" He shook his head gravely, and was non-committal. "Well, then, we've come down here to *make* you loyal, pilot!" Turning his keen eye, which had peered into many a northeaster, directly upon his interviewer, the old salt vigorously replied, "You can't make *me* loyal, for I always *have* been!" Noble words and truly spoken, as we afterwards found.

The sun was still shining brightly in the western horizon as we weighed anchor, and with colors flying and whistle sounding, steamed slowly towards the majestic bay which expands its broad bosom before the city of Charleston. The pilot, dressed in navy blue, stood at the window of the pilot-house, guiding the helmsman and announcing the various points of historic interest.

Close at hand two buoys marked the spots where the monitors "Keokuk" and "Weehawken" were sunk; and lashed to a mast-head of the latter, still visible above the water, was a small American flag floating in the breeze. But the attention of all was now suddenly arrested by a more imposing display

in the sky. For high above the city the glorious
sunset had painted the western heavens with stream-
ing bars of red and white and blue, fringed with gold.

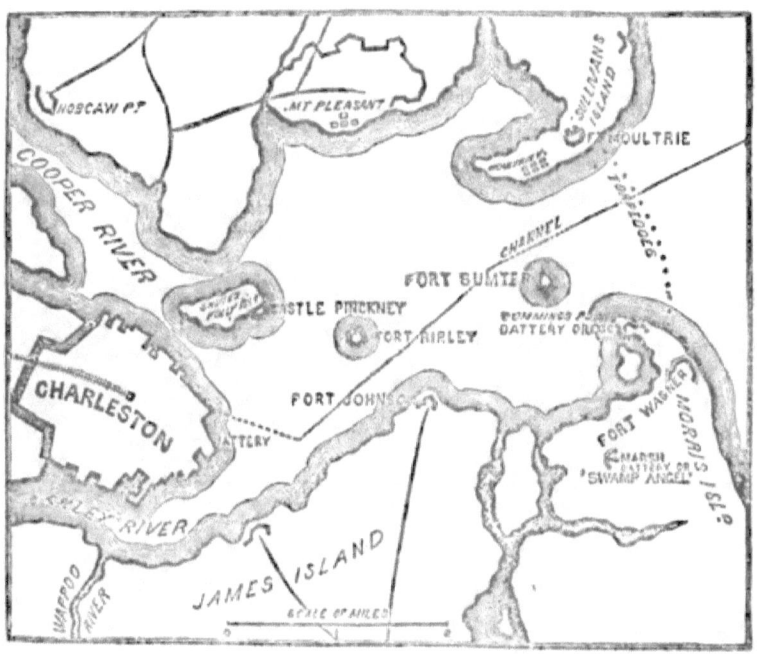

It was our banner, stretched out again by a Divine
hand, over the recovered city; and all eyes turned
to behold the sight, as the shout went up, "See, the
Red, White and Blue! The Red, White and Blue!"

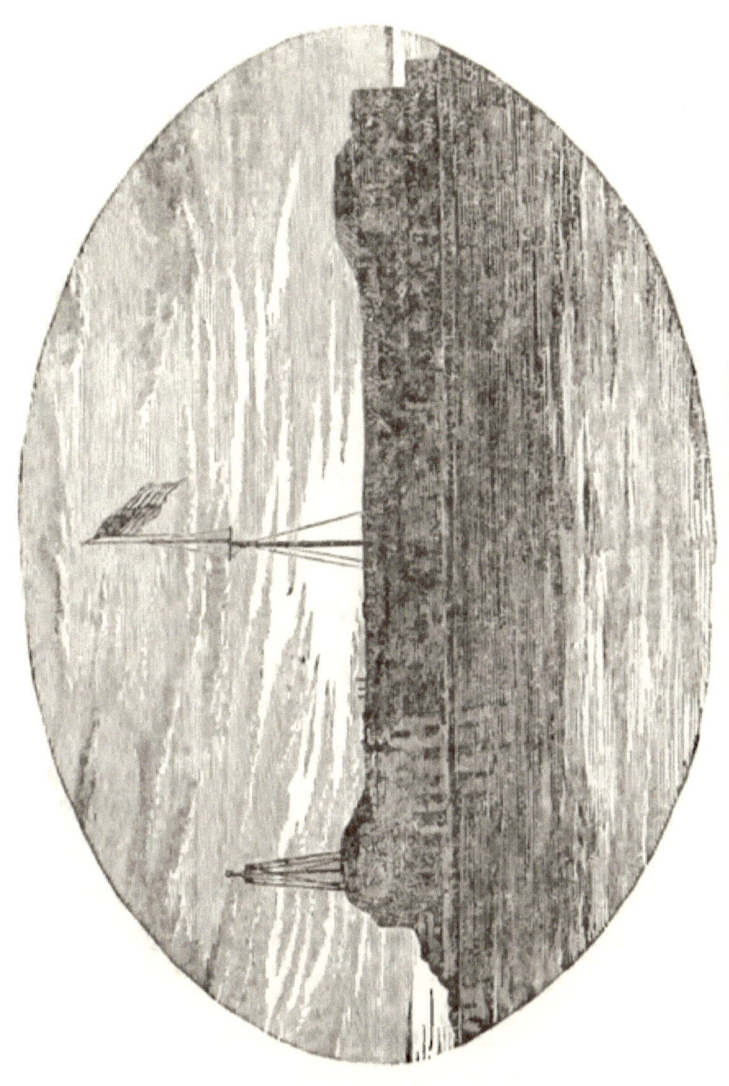

FORT SUMTER IN RUINS.

Fort Strong, formerly called Fort Wagner, on Morris Island, was passed with uncovered heads, in honor of Colonel Shaw, who fell gallantly leading his colored regiment to the assault; then Fort Putnam, formerly Battery Gregg, on Cummings' Point, and on the right Fort Moultrie and Battery Bee, on Sullivan's Island, were pointed out, till at length the cry rang out, "Fort Sumter! Fort Sumter!" Battered and crumbled almost to shapelessness, it rose before us like some vast monster in the centre of the harbor. As we drew nearer, we could distinguish the sentinels on the ramparts, whose bayonets glistened in the rays of the setting sun.

For a few moments we contemplated in silence the storied fortress, as memories of the long and bitter struggle here inaugurated passed in quick procession before us. But victory had come at last, and rebellion had perished. As by a common inspiration, all hearts and voices united in the grand old doxology,

"Praise God, from whom all blessings flow."

It was our good passport to the city, heard and honored at Fort Sumter by the rapid dipping of the colors, while the answering strains of the "Star Spangled Banner" echoed and re-echoed o'er the bay.

Passing rapidly on, we soon arrived within hailing distance of our blockading squadron, safely riding at anchor. As we gave each ship and gunboat and monitor, as we passed, the news of Lee's surrender, a scene of the wildest enthusiasm followed, which quickly spread throughout the entire fleet. The sailor boys in blue crowded to the bulwarks, or mounting aloft, manned the yards, climbing even to the main-tops, and turning swung their caps and rent the air with their shouts. "Hurrah! hurrah! Lee has surrendered! Lee has surrendered!!" How welcome the tidings after their arduous service.

"Sweet after danger 's the close of the war."

The shades of night were falling thickly about us, as we left the fleet astern and came swiftly up to the city, which was shrouded in darkness. From the midst of a crowd of people gathering on the deck ahead of us, a squeaky voice piped out, "What's the news?" and a strong voice gave back the answer:

" Lee has surrendered with his whole army!"

Again the piping voice :

"Have you got Lee?"

And the reply, with no uncertain sound :

"Yes, we've got him this time, sure," followed by an indescribable medley of southern yelling, cheering and dancing.

Amid the excitement and enthusiasm, the band of the United States steamer "Blackstone" struck up the "Star Spangled Banner," to which ours responded with "My country, 'tis of thee." Again from the "Blackstone," "The Red, White and Blue," followed by the martial notes of "Hail Columbia" from the "Oceanus" as she was made fast to the dock. Captain Hunt, of General Hatch's staff, came aboard promptly, and after exchanging congratulations over the great news, tendered us during our stay the "freedom of the city." We were not expected to avail ourselves of this courtesy till morning; a few of us, however, did get out on southern soil, just to stretch ourselves a bit after our long sea-faring, but encountering rather a suspicious looking crowd, we soon returned on board, to await the morrow, the ever-memorable fourteenth of April, 1865.

3

The day dawned at length, mild and verdant with
the breath of spring,

> "And o'er the bay,
> Slowly, in all his splendors dight,
> The great sun rises to behold the sight."

Turning toward the city we could easily distinguish
the long line of edifices along the Battery, their windows glittering in the yellow sunshine.   Quickly
dressing, we set forth on a ramble through the deserted metropolis.   There was plenty of time, as
the transports were not to leave for Fort Sumter till
ten o'clock.   Vaughan and I sauntered down East
Bay street, among the crumbling and deserted ware-
houses, to the Battery.   This was a long and straight
promenade, with stone pavement, commanding a fine
prospect of the bay and fortifications.   Here, four
years before, all was activity and bustle ; here the
populace assembled, and sent up their frenzied
shouts as the flag of the Republic was lowered, and
the ensign of Rebellion supplanted it for a season.

How changed the scene !   The streets were deserted.   The crowds were scattered and gone for-

ever! The silence of desolation reigned on every
hand, disturbed only by the songs of the summer
birds. Not even a newsboy assailed us with the
Mercury or *Courier*, containing an account of the
latest victory over the Yankees. Here, along the
Battery, were many of the finest residences, stately
mansions with broad verandas, which bore the terrible effects of the long bombardment. Their walls
were scarred and rent. The roofs were crushed, the
glass shattered, piles of rubbish and other débris
encumbered the ground, and the grass was growing
in the streets. The siege of the city had steadily
and relentlessly continued for five hundred and eighty-
eight days. It was commenced on the twenty-first
of August, 1863, by the opening of the Swamp Angel
Battery on Morris Island, five miles away. On the
seventh of September, Fort Wagner and Battery
Gregg were taken, and more guns were trained upon
the city (notably the water battery), compelling the
evacuation of the lower part. During the long siege
not less than thirteen thousand shot and shell were
thrown into the city.

We strolled into the garden of one of the deserted

mansions, which still exhibited evidences of taste and
culture, even in neglect and decay. Borders of box
lined the graveled walks and encircled beautiful
flower shrubs, or clusters of japonica, of manifold
hues; the mock-orange, the lilac and magnolia tree
were blooming luxuriantly, and grew to a remark-
able height. What a contrast to the bare gardens
we had left at home, amid a cold and cheerless storm.
We were now in another zone, in the full bloom of
summer. After helping ourselves to roses in abun-
dance, the largest I had ever seen, we passed on up
the street. Notices like the following were posted
on the doors of some of the houses: "Occupied by
permission of the Provost Marshal, the owner having
taken the oath of allegiance to the United States."
Similar cards in the shop windows announced that the
occupants had permission to transact business.

A Charleston lady complained to one of our officers, saying, "*You* treat us well enough, but *the
niggers* are *dreadful* sassy. They don't turn out
now when you meet them; they even smoke cigars,
and go right up to a gentleman and ask him for a
light!"

We now began to meet contrabands of all ages and of all sizes, from the little barefooted piccaninnies and chimney sweeps to the old, gray-haired uncles and turbaned aunties. While all appeared bubbling over with joy, yet they were quiet and orderly, greeting us with bows and courtesies, and a "God bress ye! we're so powerful glad ye've come!" Said one old negro to another, "Yer mus' try now, an' do as yer done by, Uncle Rube." "Yeth," said Uncle Reuben, "but de fact am *dis* chile ain't never been *done by!* Dat's where de shoe pinches!"

We took great pleasure in calling with other friends upon Colonel Lorenzo Potter, one of the veteran Union citizens, formerly of Providence. He had been at home only a few weeks, but his family had remained through the long and dreary siege. Fortunately the shells from the Union batteries had spared the home of these devoted loyalists.

I remember a fine fig-tree in his garden, laden with fruit, and my disappointment at finding it in a green state, "for the time of figs was not yet." Reluctantly leaving this hospitable family, we made a hasty tour of several public buildings and banks, which we found in a sadly *broken* and ravaged condition. The elaborately carved counters and wainscoting had been reduced to fragments ; the tiled floors and frescoed walls were plowed up and ruined by exploding shells. In one of the banks I secured a collection of both Continental and Confederate notes, the obsolete currency of two centuries. On one of them I read this curious endorsement : "Payable two years after a treaty of peace between the Confederate and United States Governments." But right before me lay the effective protest of the Union shot and shell

against any treaty of peace with armed rebellion, in
the shape of an immense pile of débris,—broken
brick and glass, and charred timbers, the ruins of a
once fine and imposing structure. I was told of an
estimable lady of Charleston who, after investing her
all (fully $5,000) in these Confederate "promises to
pay," brought them out at last, and kindled her
morning fire with the worthless chaff. Most of the
citizens who were considered wealthy at the beginning of the war were reduced to penury at its close,
and were to be seen carrying their rations through
the streets of Charleston.

"General Wade Hampton needs horses," read the
last order of the Governor to the citizens, on the
twenty-first of January, 1865, "and I have told him
he shall have them. Put aside your please-car-
riages for the time, and bring or send in your horses
to Columbia. Colonel C. T. Hampton is charged
by me with the duty of receiving with thanks all
that will be sent, and of *taking* all that are withheld.
The horses will be paid for. No one shall suffer
from his devotion to the State."

The public conveyances kindly placed at our disposal by the authorities, showed how effectively this order had been carried out. Such a sorry looking set of horses, mules and donkeys, attached to omnibuses, army ambulances and fish-wagons, would appropriately have found a place in a Providence Antique and Horrible procession!

Passing on to the Market Building we stopped to chat with the darkey shop-keepers who occupied the few stalls which were open. We purchased here some sugar-cane and strawberries, the first of the season. The darkeys proved to be pretty shrewd traders, and promptly declined all offers of Confederate currency in payment. One shook his woolly head, saying, "O, sar, we'd better *gib* um to you, sar!" They had evidently acquired some of the sharpness of their old masters, one of whom I read about used to make his negroes *whistle* while they were picking cherries, for fear they would *eat* some! But now they could sing their Jubilee hymn, as their colored brethren sung it, marching through Richmond :

" De whip is lost, de han'cuf broken,
   An' massa 'l hab to *whistle* for his *pay;*
   He's ole enough, big enough, an' ought to known better
   Dan to went an' run'd away :
            Ole massa run, ha! ha!
            De darkey stay, ho! ho!
            It mus' be now dat de kingdom's cummin',
            An' de year of Jubilo!"

Some ragged negro boys on the street, who, by
the way they danced, appeared to have india-rubber
joints, and who ended their songs with a "shout"
and a "break-down," were asked if they knew the
John Brown song.

"Oh, yeth, massa ; we know ole John Brown."

"Well, give it to us then."

   " John Brown's body lies a mold'ring in de clay,
     But his soul am a marchin' home!"

"Good! give us some more!"

   " We'll hang Jeff Davis on a sour apple tree,
     On Canaan's happy *sho'*!"

Some of them doubtless still sing the new version,
believing that Jeff Davis will yet be hung, on Canaan's happy shore ; and so they are all "bound for

the happy land of Canaan!" It has been stated as an indisputable *fact*, that some of the older negroes having never heard their masters mention the name of a Yankee except with a profane accompaniment, have been praying for years, "O Lord! bress, we beseech Thee, and speedily bring along de comin' of de *dam* Yankees!"

Retracing our steps towards the steamer, we met our friends coming from various directions. Some of them would have passed for returning miners, who, in lieu of rich booty, were heavily laden with relics of stone, brass and iron. While these Yankee relic-hunters failed in getting away with old Fort Sumter itself, they successfully carried off two six-hundred pound shots from the great English Blakely gun, (sent over to the rebels by friends in England.) They afterwards presented these to the New York and Long Island Historical Societies, as enduring evidences of British neutrality during our war.

My mementoes included *several hundred dollars worth*, so to speak, of Confederate currency; a tile from the floor of the State Bank of South Carolina, and a Book of Common Prayer picked up among the

Ruins of Circular Church. St. Michael's Church. Ruins of Institute Hall.

CHARLESTON IN RUINS.

rubbish in St. Michael's Episcopal Church. The floor of the edifice was covered with the shattered glass from the windows. A large shell had ploughed its way directly through the tower, fragments passing through the rear wall of the church, demolishing the pulpit, and even "breaking the commandments" inscribed on tablets attached to the wall. But the iron messenger kindly spared the precepts most needed in Charleston, "Thou shalt not kill!" and "Thou shalt not steal!"

We climbed to the top of the tower of this ancient structure, whose chimes had been removed to be recast into rebel cannon. I have since heard that a new set of chimes now ring out the glad notes of Freedom.

Near by, on the right, were the ruins of Institute Hall, where the Ordinance of Secession was passed, December 20th, 1860, by more than five hundred majority. On the left, the ruins of Circular Church, where the first secession sermon was preached.

But the hour for the grand ceremonial at Sumter had now almost arrived. Hastily embarking on the transport "Golden Gate," the brilliant pageant in the

4

harbor opened before us. As far as the eye could reach, its waters were thickly crowded with shipping, gaily decked from bow-sprit to yard-arm and top-mast, "with flags and streamers gay, in honor of the gala-day!" While on every ship and transport, in every available place, were assembled the expectant multitude.

A steamer in the advance suddenly attracted our attention, decked with banners and crowded with the boys in blue. Can it be? Yes, it is our old Rhode Island steamer "Canonicus." Summoned at the opening of the war from the peaceful waters of Narragansett bay, she had rendered efficient service as a government transport, and now at its close had been honorably chosen to lead the grand procession in the peaceful advance to Fort Sumter. Presently the signal was given, the drums were beaten, the trumpets sounded, and immediately the "Canonicus" led the proud procession, followed by a long line of steamers and transports which gracefully rounded into line. Prominent among them was the "Planter," commanded by Robert Small, a freedman, who shouted his orders from the top of the paddle-box, while all around him, and below, in every nook and corner, were crowded the happy contrabands of South Carolina, of all ages and sizes, presenting in their variety of costumes a most novel and fantastic picture.

It was a proud day for them and for Robert Small, who, a few months before, almost unaided and alone, had captured the "Planter" from the armed State of South Carolina, safely passed the rebel batteries, and delivered her a prize to our blockaders. He received from the government $4,500, one-half the value of the steamer, with a commission of $1,800 as her commander. He afterwards purchased his old master's house and furniture, which set him up as immensely rich among his people, who declared him to be "de dun smartest cullud man in Souf Curlina !"

As the long procession of steamers and transports passed the fleet at anchor, manned and decked most gallantly, there was a scene of indescribable enthusiasm ; guns were booming, bands playing triumphal marches, bells ringing and whistles sounding, while everybody was shouting and cheering at the highest

pitch of patriotic exultation. This continued una-
bated till we reached the landing of Fort Sumter.
Disembarking we passed between two files of soldiers, black men on the right, and white men on
the left, rivalling each other in soldierly bearing.
Ascending a flight of fifty steps we reached the parapet of the fort, where we found the Rhode Island
boys of Company B, Third Artillery, Lieutenant J.
E. Burroughs commanding, in charge of six pieces
of artillery. Captain J. M. Barker and his men, of
Company D, were on duty on Morris Island; and
our comrade, Charles H. Williams, with a detach-
ment of Company B, were on Sullivan's Island,
in charge of Fort Moultrie and Battery Bee. As
I stood there on the parapet of Sumter, and looked
out over the battered and crumbled fortress, I real-
ized how it had become, even in ruins, well nigh
impregnable. The upper, or barbette walls, had
fallen on the outside, and lay packed solidly against
the lower walls, choking the entrances to the shattered casemates; numberless great guns, whose thun-
der had long been the voice of battle, lay dismounted
and half buried in the sand, while the immense vol-

ume of shot and shell which had been hurled against
the fort had served only to solidify and strengthen
the entire mass.   The fort was further protected from
a scaling party by *cheveaux de frise* of pointed pick-
ets, while along the base of the wall, near the water
line, was a barrier of interlaced wire fence, invisible
at the distance of a few feet, and which effectively
resisted the advance of our naval forces on the night
of September 8, 1863.

In the interior of the fort, packed tier above tier
against the walls, were layers of tall wicker baskets
filled with sand.   In the centre stood the new flag-
staff, nearly one hundred and fifty feet high, while
here and there, at considerable intervals, were piled
pyramids of solid shot.

But the grim aspect of war had been somewhat
softened by the floral decorations, which, I was
informed, were the combined taste of six Union ladies
of Charleston.   Near the flag-staff, a graceful arched
canopy had been erected, draped with the American
flag, and handsomely trimmed with evergreens and
myrtle.   On the stage beside the speakers' stand,
was a golden eagle, resting upon a shield of the

national colors, and holding in his beak a wreath of
flowers and evergreen.

Descending to the interior of the fort, we passed
from the foot of the wall-steps to the platform
through a double file of navy boys, in trimmest holi-
day attire. Here were now assembled the great
audience of five thousand soldiers, sailors and citizens, and we joined them in the stirring song of
"Victory at Last," composed for the occasion by William B. Bradbury, who was present and led the singing. Then followed the old battle song :

> "Yes, we'll rally round the flag, boys, rally once again,
>   Shouting the battle-cry of Freedom."

The formal exercises were opened with prayer by
the Rev. Matthias Harris, Chaplain United States
Army, a venerable man, who had made the prayer
at the raising of the flag on Fort Sumter, in December, 1860, when Major Anderson removed his command from Fort Moultrie. It was a brief but touch-
ing invocation for the blessing of God upon the flag
of the nation, and upon the great occasion. The
Rev. R. S. Storrs, D. D., of Brooklyn, N. Y., then

read with the audience, alternately, the one hundred and twenty-sixth, forty-seventh, ninety-eighth, and a part of the twentieth Psalms.

Major Anderson's dispatch to the Government, April 18, 1861, on steamship "Baltic," off Sandy Hook, announcing the fall of Fort Sumter, was then read by Brigadier-General E. D. Townshend, Assistant Adjutant-General United States Army.

Then came the crowning event of the day, the "raising and planting upon the ruins of Fort Sumter of the SAME United States flag which floated over the battlements of the fort during the rebel assault, April 14, 1861, by Brevet Major-General Robert Anderson, United States Army."

Promptly upon the reading of the dispatch, Sergeant Hart (who had gallantly replaced the flag after it had been shot away in the first assault) stepped forward with the Fort Sumter mail-bag in his hand. As he quietly drew forth from its long seclusion the *same* old flag of '61, a wild shout went up, "prolonged and loud." It was quickly attached to the halyards by three sailors from the fleet, who were in the first fight, and crowned with a wreath of evergreen, set with clusters of rosebuds and orange blossoms.

All was now ready, and the hour, the moment, for which the nation had so long earnestly struggled and patiently waited, had come at last !

"Though the mills of God grind slowly,
    Yet they grind exceeding small;
Though with patience He stands waiting,
    With exactness grinds He all!"

ROBERT ANDERSON.

Who of us can ever forget that memorable hour, or the deep and silent expectation of the great assembly, as General Robert Anderson, the hero of the day, stepped forward, and with uncovered head and a voice trembling with emotion, said :

"I am here, my friends, my fellow-citizens and fellow-soldiers, to perform an act of duty to my country, dear to my heart, and which all of you will appreciate and feel. Had I observed the wishes of my heart, it should have been done in silence ; but in accordance with the request of the Honorable Secretary of War, I make a few remarks, as by his order, after four long, long years of war, I

THE FLAG REPLACED ON SUMTER.

restore to its proper place this dear flag, which floated here during
peace, before the first act of this cruel rebellion. [Taking the halyards in his hands, he said:] I thank God that I have lived to see
this day, and to be here, to perform this, perhaps the last act of my
life, of duty to my country. My heart is filled with gratitude to
that God who has so signally blessed us, who has given us blessings beyond measure. May all the nations bless and praise the
name of the Lord, and all the world proclaim, 'Glory to God in the
highest, and on earth peace, good will toward men.' "

"Amen! amen!" the multitude responded. Then
the old veteran grasped the halyards with firm and
steady hand, and

> " Forthwith from the glittering staff unfurled
> The starry banner, which full high advanced,
> Shone like a meteor streaming to the wind."

A loud and prolonged shout, from fort and fleet,
greeted the old flag as, all tattered with shot and
shell, it rose above the battlements into its native air.
The whole audience sprang to their feet. Several
bands began to play their most inspiring music.
Men swung their hats and grasped each other by
the hand; women and children waved their hand-
kerchiefs, and many wept for very joy. As it rested
at length in its old place at the top of the staff, and
waved its victorious folds towards the recovered city,

which had first disowned it, the enthusiasm became
tumultuous and overpowering, till at last it found
relief in the national song :

> "The star spangled banner, O long may it wave,
>   O'er the land of the free, and the home of the brave! "

I can never forget the impression of that glorious
spectacle, and that song of victory that went up from
five thousand voices. The colored soldier pacing,
to and fro, with beating heart and gazing aloft with
pride upon the "flag of the free hearts' hope and
home," could now exclaim, "Yes, that is now *my*
flag ! and yonder, at Fort Wagner, the colored soldier
fought and died to restore it.   Four years ago, when
that flag went down, more than four millions of my
people *had* no flag !   But to-day it is *our* flag, and
our country !"

Immediately followed the grand artillery salute to
the flag ; and I left my seat and climbed the look-out
high above upon the wall to obtain an unobstructed
view of the bay.   First, the heavy guns of Sumter
thundered forth their hearty greeting to the flag.
Then, in loyal and quick response, came the an-

swering notes from Fort Moultrie and Morris Island, followed by a national salute from every fort and rebel battery that had fired upon the flag four years before.

Finally the fleet, with the little monitors, joined in the deep harmonies of the grand chorus, till the earth trembled with the cannonade, the air grew heavy with smoke, and nothing was visible but the rapid flashes of the artillery. For a moment it seemed as if the assault of '61 was being re-enacted before me. But it is safe to add that had this been the case, I should hardly have chosen such an elevated position upon the observatory of the fort. At length the roar of cannon ceased, the dense clouds of smoke and sand drifted away, and order was restored. The orator of the day, Rev. Henry Ward Beecher, then began his address, of which the opening and closing sentences were as follows:

"On this solemn and joyful day, we again lift to the breeze our fathers' flag, now, again, the banner of *the United States*, with the fervent prayer that God would crown it with honor, protect it from treason, and send it down to our children, with all the blessings of civilization, liberty and religion. Terrible in battle, may it be beneficent in peace. Happily, no bird or beast of prey has been

5

inscribed upon it. The stars that redeem the night from darkness,
and the beams of red light that beautify the morning, have been
united upon its folds. As long as the sun endures, or the stars,
may it wave over a nation neither enslaved nor enslaving. [Great
applause.]

"Once, and but once, has treason dishonored it. In that insane
hour, when the guiltiest and bloodiest rebellion of time hurled their
fires upon this fort, you, sir, [turning to General Anderson,] and a
small, heroic band, stood within these now crumbled walls, and did
gallant and just battle for the honor and defense of the nation's
banner. [Applause.]

*   *   *   *   *   *   *   *   *

"To-day you are returned again. We devoutly join with you in
thanksgiving to Almighty God, that he has spared your honored
life, and vouchsafed you the honors of this day. The heavens over
you are the same; the same shores; morning comes, and evening,
as they did. All else, how changed! What grim batteries crowd
the burdened shores! What scenes have filled this air, and disturbed these waters! These shattered heaps of shapeless stone are
all that is left of Fort Sumter. Desolation broods in yonder sad
city—solemn retribution hath avenged our dishonored banner!
You have come back with honor, who departed hence, four years
ago, leaving the air sultry with fanaticism. The surging crowds
that rolled up their frenzied shouts, as the flag came down, are
dead, or scattered, or silent; and their habitations are desolate.
Ruin sits in the cradle of treason. Rebellion has perished. But
there flies the same flag that was insulted. [Great and prolonged
applause.] With starry eyes it looks all over this bay for that banner that supplanted it, and sees it not. [Applause.] You that then,
for the day, were humbled, are here again, to triumph once and
forever. [Applause.] In the storm of that assault this glorious

ensign was often struck; but, memorable fact, not one of its *stars*
was torn out by shot or shell. [Applause.] It was a prophecy. It
said, 'Not one State shall be struck from this nation by treason!'
The fulfillment is at hand. Lifted to the air, to-day, it proclaims,
after four years of war, 'Not a State is blotted out!' [Applause.]
Hail to the flag of our fathers, and our flag! Glory to the banner
that has gone through four years black with tempests of war, to
pilot the nation back to peace without dismemberment! And glory
be to God, who, above all hosts and banners, hath ordained victory,
and shall ordain peace! [Applause.]

"Our nation, under one government, without slavery, has been
ordained, and shall stand. There can be peace on no other basis.
Reverently, piously, in hopeful patriotism, we spread this banner
on the sky, as of old the bow was planted on the cloud; and, with
solemn fervor, beseech God to look upon it, and make it the memo-
rial of an everlasting covenant and decree, that never again on this
fair land shall a deluge of blood prevail. [Applause.]

  * * * * * * * * *

"From this pulpit of broken stone we speak forth our earnest
greeting to all our land.

"We offer to the President of these United States our solemn
congratulations that God has sustained his life and health under
the unparalleled burdens and sufferings of four bloody years, and
permitted him to behold this auspicious consummation of that
national unity for which he has waited with so much patience and
fortitude, and for which he has labored with such disinterested
wisdom. [Applause.]

"To the members of the government associated with him in the
administration of perilous affairs in critical times; to the Senators
and Representatives of the United States, who have eagerly fash-

ioned the instruments by which the popular will might express and
enforce itself, we tender our grateful thanks. [Applause.]

"To the officers and men of the Army and Navy, who have so
faithfully, skillfully, and gloriously upheld their country's authority, by suffering, labor, and sublime courage, we offer here a tribute
beyond the compass of words. [Great applause.]

"Upon these true and faithful citizens, men and women, who
have borne up with unflinching hope in the darkest hour, and covered the land with the labors of love and charity, we invoke the
divinest blessing of Him whom they have so truly imitated.
[Applause.]

"But, chiefly, to Thee, God of our fathers, we render thanksgiving and praise for that wondrous Providence that has brought forth
from such a harvest of war, the seed of so much liberty and peace.
We invoke peace upon the North. Peace be to the West. Peace
be upon the South.

"In the name of God we lift up our banner, and dedicate it to
Peace, Union and Liberty, now and forever." [Great applause.]

At the conclusion of the address, the audience
arose and sang the doxology. An impressive prayer
followed, with the benediction, by the Rev. Dr.
Storrs, Jr. Six deafening cheers were then given
for the old flag replaced on Sumter; and three
times three for President Lincoln, General Robert
Anderson, and our soldiers and sailors. Many of
us remained to avail ourselves of the opportunity to
shake hands with the old veteran, and I well remem-

ber the exultation with which I walked off with the
General's autograph.

We spent an hour in exploring the walls and case-
ments of the fort and rummaging about for relics.
It was amusing to see a man who, after selecting a
twenty-five pound shot for a memento, would carry
it a short distance, change hands to make it easier,
and then come to the conclusion that it was foolish
to lug such a heavy thing around ; or to see another
person, who had been sweating under the burden
of a heavy shell,— when suddenly told that it was
still loaded and liable to go off, and take him off with
it,— quickly turn and lay it down carefully, and
quietly depart. I satisfied my curiosity with a few
small grape and canister shot, some fragments of
exploded shells, and a section of the rebel iron wire
fence on the outer wall.

It must have been fully six o'clock when we all
arrived safely back to the city. At sunset there was
another grand salute from the fleet, and in the evening we were summoned on deck to witness the closing demonstration of the day. Nothing could be
seen in the darkness, till quick, as if by magic, at

the signal from the flag-ship of the Admiral, the
entire harbor for miles around was brilliantly illuminated.   Every vessel and transport and monitor
was ablaze with many-colored fires.   Each mast and
sail and rope was aglow with light.   From every
deck came the roar and glare of rockets, darting in
quick procession to the sky, then turning and
descending in showers of golden rain. · Hundreds of
lanterns, red, green and white, suspended from the
rigging, flashed out their starry signals over the bay,
and were reflected in the waters beneath, while heavy
clouds of smoke, tinged with golden radiance, rolled
heavenward like ascending incense, presenting a
scene of rare enchantment.

But hark! another signal gun is heard.   Every
light instantly disappears!   Every sound is hushed!
and grim darkness again mantles the waters of the
bay ; and, I was about to add, we were all soon in
sleep's serene oblivion, but my diary records that at
nine o'clock P. M. five of us took an impressed carriage and started for the Charleston Hotel, to attend
a reception given by General Gilmore.   On our arri-
val, we made a bargain with our negro driver to wait

for us, say half an hour, more or less, and then take
us over to the Battery, to General Hatch's grand
military ball.   But once inside, we became so much
absorbed, like little Tommy Tucker, in the supper
and the toasts, that we forgot all about our colored
driver outside,—just as people do at parties still.
The following are brief extracts from the remarks of
two or three of the principal speakers.

Judge-Advocate Holt, in responding to the toast,
"General Robert Anderson," said :

"It is not uncommon for organizations in treason or in crime,
on a vast scale, to commit mistakes in the selection of agents to
accomplish their work ; and no man in all history committed a
greater mistake than Floyd, in the selection of General Anderson,
on the sole ground of his being a southern man, to command Fort
Sumter. He thought to find in him a tool of treason, but he found
instead a loyal, fearless, and true man. Those who have led great
treasonable enterprises, or great crimes, have suffered most from
mingled rage and angry fear when they discovered such mistakes
in the selection of their agents, and none suffered more in this
respect than Secretary Floyd, on hearing of the transfer of the small
but devoted garrison from Fort Moultrie to the solid walls of Fort
Sumter. There was one man, still in the service of the government, who was with Floyd, in the Cabinet, at the time, and could
bear evidence to the rage of the defeated traitor, and that man, with
giant brain and steadfast heart, has for three years presided at the
head of the War Department—Edwin M. Stanton."

Major-General Abner Doubleday was called out by some remarks referring to the part he took in the defense of Fort Sumter, and said :

"I feel to-day as if I had been present at the birth of a new nation. I was most happy to have been present at the impressive ceremonies this day, and glad to remember that I dealt some blows against secession in the same place four years ago. I never doubted then the propriety of our resistance. I felt that the only answer to armed treason must come from the mouth of the cannon. There is one class of men in that early effort to whom justice has not been done. I mean the enlisted men. They were offered every inducement to desert,—heavy bribes, and promotion in a new service,—but they refused them all. [Cheers.] They were told that there would be no necessity for any fighting; that there would soon be peace, as the North could not stand up against them; but all their efforts failed, and I give you, 'The remembrance of those noble soldiers.'" [Great cheering.]

But we were particularly interested in General Robert Anderson's response to a toast which had been assigned to General John A. Dix, who sent the famous order to Louisiana, in 1861, "If any man attempts to haul down the American flag, shoot him on the spot ! "

General Anderson concluded by introducing the toast, "Abraham Lincoln," with an eloquent tribute of respect and affection. Said he :

"I beg you now, that you will join me in drinking the health of another man whom we all love to honor,—the man who, when elected President of the United States, was compelled to reach the seat of government without an escort, but a man who now could travel *all* over our country with millions of hands and hearts to sustain him. I give you the good, the great, the honest man, Abraham Lincoln."

How little we dreamed, as the cheers, twice repeated, went around, that at that self-same hour the honored President lay prostrate and dying in the National Capital from the bullet of an assassin.

"Thus grief ever treads upon the heels of pleasure"—
"And all alike await the inevitable hour;
  The paths of glory lead but to the grave."

Having now remained at the hotel over an hour, we went out to look after our colored coachman, only to find, as we might have expected, that he had given us the slip. But we took possession of another carriage that fortunately came up, and, in answer to the sable inquiry, "Am Colonel Fuller ready for de ball?" we kindly informed our colored friend that if he would take us to the ball, the Colonel would undoubtedly be ready by the time he returned. Thus assured, he started off with us over a very dark and rough road,

through the burnt district, till we stopped at length
before a fine old mansion on East Bay street, brilliantly illuminated, from which sounds of music and
festivity proceeded.   Here, we were told, was the
scene of another grand ball, given by the Confederates in honor of the fall of Sumter, just four years
before.   Some of the same negroes who served at
the first ball, as *slaves*, now attended the second as
free and independent waiters.   I purchased of one of
them for a nominal sum quite a collection of Confederate currency, a Palmetto brass button, and a quaint
Pompeiian lamp, which are still preserved as mementoes of the occasion.   We were told " dat Massa
Middleton used to own de place," but, as the darkeys
sing :

> " He saw a smoke way down de ribber,
>   Where de Lincum gunboats lay,
>   He took his hat, an' lef' berry sudden,
>   An' I 'specs he's run'd away!"

So the fine estate, with its broad verandas, and
elegant mirrors and paintings on the walls, all became, including the darkeys, " contraband of war."

The next day was Saturday, and it was announced
that the " Oceanus " would sail at five in the after-

noon. The hour of departure was afterwards post-
poned to Sunday morning at nine o'clock, by advice
of the pilot. We visited various points of interest
on Saturday, including the office of the Charleston
Mercury, where we secured some interesting papers,
which are referred to in the Appendix. We also
saw the slave-marts, where families had so long been
bought and sold like cattle. I secured a bill of sale
of a slave who was described as
"a negro fellow called Simon."
The seller's name was Mordecai,
and the buyer of "the sole use of
Simon forever," was a Mr. Laz-
arus.

During the morning, one of
our lady passengers was accosted
by an aged black woman with a
hen and a bag of eggs, as follows : "Missus, I want to gib
de northern ladies sumthin', but
I have nuthin' but this yer hen,
and these yer eggs. Won't you
take 'em ?" This was too much

for the sympathetic nature of Mrs. B——, but what
to do with the hen and her products so far from home,
was the question. Finally the eggs were taken and
the hen left. The woman was rewarded and departed in much delight. On the homeward voyage
a gentleman proposed to take them up to his country seat in New York State, and put them under the
care of the most motherly hen of his large flock.
This was done with the following result :

"JUNE 10, 1865.

"I am happy to inform you that the Charleston hen has done her
duty as well as could be expected under the circumstances. The
eggs were evidently the product of secession times, and stoutly
resisted all northern influences. But the mother hen dertermined,
'a la General Grant,' to set it out on this nest 'if it took all summer!' A great destruction of capital has been the result, but
'victory at last' has rewarded her efforts, and she is now followed
by a train of four bipeds, one black, one white, and two octoroons.
I have neglected to tell you that the mother hen is black, and struts
with pompous pride above her white and octoroon subjects. 'Let
us have peace.' "

My record would be incomplete without a brief
description of the freedmen's meetings on Saturday.
We found Citadel square almost impassable with the
dense crowds of negroes, while hundreds of children

were marching through the streets singing "John Brown." The principal gathering was in Zion's Church, where more than three thousand colored people were crowded together. One of the speakers from the north, William Lloyd Garrison, the veteran abolitionist, was surrounded by the freedmen as he entered the church, and borne on their shoulders amid great enthusiasm to the platform. Then the surging multitude sang, with thrilling power and effect :

"Roll, Jordan, roll, the year of Jubilee;"

and another song, beginning :

"Blow, blow your trumpet, Gabriel!"

How they all shouted at the first mention of the name of Lincoln! "Spread it abroad," said Hon. Henry Wilson, "all over South Carolina, that the black men of South Carolina know no master now, and that they are slaves no more forever! [Great cheering.] Abraham Lincoln, President of the United States [tremendous cheering and waving of hats and handkerchiefs], with twenty-five millions of freemen by his side, and seven hundred thousand bayonets

6

behind him, has decreed it, and it will stand while
the world stands, that the black men of South Carolina can never more be slaves! [Loud cheers.]
They have robbed your cradles; they have sold your
children; they have separated husband and wife,
father and mother and child. [Cries of 'Yes! yes!
yes!'] They shall separate you no more! ['Halle-
lujah! bress de Lord!'] The long, dreary night of
slavery has passed away forever. ['Amen! amen!
amen!'] Remember that you are now to be obe-
dient, faithful, true and loyal to your country for-
evermore!" [Cheers and cries of 'Yes! yes! yes!']

Twenty years have passed since the emancipation
of this race, and while a great work has been accom-
plished for their education, aided by the princely
gifts of such philanthropists as George Peabody and
John F. Slater, of New England, it is also true that
much remains to be done. There still appears to
exist among the ruling class in the south a tendency
to put barriers in the way of the poor and ignorant
masses, and hinder them in the exercise of their per-
sonal and political rights. "This is a white man's
government," exclaims the solid south to-day, as in

(Copyrighted by J. A. & R. A. Reid.)

"OLE MASSA RUN—HA! HA!
DE DARKEYS STAY—HO! HO!"

1860. And again let the loyal answer go forth, as
from the lips of the lamented Lincoln, at Gettysburg,
twenty years ago, "This is a government of the people, by the people, and for the people, without dis-
tinction of race or color." The most serious danger
which threatens our country to-day, is the ignorance
of the masses, both white and black, north as well as
south. This class in many States holds the balance
of power, and has become a most dangerous force in
the hands of educated but unprincipled leaders.
The beneficent influences of Christianity and universal education are necessary to lift the masses from
their servile position, and enable them to think and
vote for themselves. Nor should they be allowed to
vote until they can read and write. Education and
suffrage should go hand in hand.

CONCLUSION.

On the morning of Sunday, the sixteenth of April,
1865, the good steamer "Oceanus," gay with crowds
of passengers, and proudly waving flags and signals,
steamed slowly down Charleston harbor homeward
bound. As she passed the fleet, parting salutations

were exchanged with the monitors, men-of-war, and the smaller boats passing to and fro. We turned to take a last survey of the city in the distance, the forts, and shores thickly studded with now peaceful batteries. As we passed abreast of Fort Sumter, where, as at Lexington a hundred years ago, "was fired the shot heard 'round the world," every head was uncovered, while we reverently sang, the band accompanying:

"Praise God, from whom all blessings flow,"

followed by the sweet strains of:

"My country, 'tis of thee,
Sweet land of liberty."

Immediately the colors on the fort were dipped, and the sentinels on the walls waved their adieus with caps and bayonets. At length we crossed the bar and took leave of the pilot.

As the shores of South Carolina faded in the distance, and the walls of the storied fort sank below the gray horizon, we bade farewell to scenes which, however changed by the ceaseless march of time, must always possess a charm indescribable. Religious services were held in the cabin at eleven o'clock, and again during the evening. The sound of merriment was hushed, and all seemed to realize that it was the Sabbath. Indeed, it was observed by one of the speakers, that he had not heard a word of profanity or seen any one under the influence of intoxicating beverages during the voyage.

Monday followed without important incident, save that at five o'clock in the afternoon we safely rounded Cape Hatteras with a gentle reminder of the old couplet :

> "If the Bermudas let you pass,
> You must beware of Hatteras !"

Tuesday morning, when about thirty miles south of Fortress Monroe, and while most of the passengers were at breakfast, a steamer was observed in the distance with her flag at half-mast. Various were the conjectures for whom it could be. We had been without news from the north for more than a week ; what could have happened?

Presently a pilot-boat, with her colors also at half-mast, appeared within hailing distance.

"What's the news?" was eagerly shouted from the "Oceanus."

ABRAHAM LINCOLN.

"The President is dead," came faintly back, with startling effect, over the water. Immediately the breakfast tables were deserted, and the passengers gathered in astonished groups on deck, exclaiming, "It cannot be!" "We do not believe it!" But a second pilot-boat could now be seen with her flag, half-hoisted, drooping from the halyards. Again the earnest inquiry, "What's the news?"

"President Lincoln is dead."

"How did he die?"

"He was assassinated in Washington."

Then stout hearts trembled with dismay, and men unused to tears turned pale and wept. As we passed vessel after vessel, we obtained further particulars of the cruel tragedy, and the feeling of gloom and indignation which prevailed was deep and indescribable.

Nothing else was thought or talked of, till we arrived
at the fortress. On landing, I purchased a Richmond paper, containing a full account of the assassi-
nation, the murderous attack upon Secretary Seward
and his sons, with the plot to remove General Grant
and the entire Cabinet. We found the entrance to
the fortress draped in mourning, and the saddest
reminders of all were the portraits of the departed
President, deeply hung with crape, in the various
offices. We made but a brief stay at the splendid
fortress, with its powerful armament, where, a few
weeks later, Jefferson Davis was brought and confined
as a prisoner of war. We could plainly discern "the
Rip Raps" and Sewall's Point, and the locality was
pointed out "in the Roads," where the little Monitor
defeated the Merrimac, in 1862, and saved the Union
fleet. The story of this famous battle, and the rev-
olution it produced in naval warfare, has been graph-
ically recited by Comrade F. B. Butts.

But the sad intelligence from the Capital had
crushed the desire for sight-seeing, and all seemed
anxious to get home with the least possible delay.
After taking a supply of coal and water, and landing

four or five blockade-runners who had secreted them-selves in our coal-bunkers at Charleston, we were again "homeward bound."

Wednesday morning found us well on our voyage to New York, with continued pleasant weather. At half-past ten, the Sumter Club, which had been organized, held a meeting, and the rebel flag of Fort Moultrie was formally presented to the Club. It was voted to procure a suitable gold badge, with Fort Sumter engraved upon it, for each member. It was further voted that every passenger who sailed from New York for Charleston on the "Oceanus" should be entitled to membership.

Appropriate services were held on board at eleven o'clock, the hour at which the funeral obsequies of the President were being solemnized in Washington.

At three o'clock we were opposite Coney Island, and entering the Narrows. After a short detention at quarantine, we rapidly passed the light-houses and forts and the fleet of shipping, moving and at an-chor about the great metropolis, and drew into the dock at the foot of Robinson street as the city bells struck five. Hasty farewells were exchanged with

friends on board, mingled with greetings from friends
on shore. Making my way with difficulty through
the crowds of people and among teams, drays and
carriages, I at length emerged into the streets of
New York.

But what a change! The city was in mourning!
Ten days before, every highway and avenue had
been resplendent with flags and streamers; and a
whole city had celebrated with joy and thanksgiving the return of peace and the triumph of loyalty
over armed rebellion. We had sailed to the metropolis of the south, the Cradle of the Rebellion, and
found it a city in ruins. There, where the national
ensign had been first dishonored, we had seen it
uplifted and restored with imposing ceremonies, amid
the shouts of a race redeemed and set free. To-day
we had returned to find New York as mournful as
Charleston. A national calamity had filled the land
with mourning. From every flag-staff the "stars
and stripes," shrouded in black, drooped at half-mast.
From the houses of rich and poor alike, hung the
emblems of the universal sorrow. It is estimated that
not less than five hundred thousand people, the rep-

resentatives of all classes, crowded the entrances to
the City Hall to take a last look at the familiar fea-
tures of the beloved President, who had so endeared
himself to all parties by his patience, wisdom and
fidelity during his long and difficult term of service.
Just before the fall of Richmond he uttered those
ever-memorable words, his fitting epitaph : " With
malice towards none, with charity for all, with firm-
ness in the right, as God gives us to see the right,
let us strive to finish the work we are in, and do all
which may achieve and cherish a just and a lasting
peace among ourselves and with all nations." His
work was finished. The nation was reunited, and
at peace with all the world. As we enjoy to-day
the blessings of peace and orderly progress let us
never forget the name of Lincoln. Let us ever
remember at what a fearful sacrifice of precious blood
and treasure, Liberty and Union were maintained,
and "the flag replaced on Sumter."

VICTORY AT LAST.

SONG AND CHORUS.

Words by Mrs. M. A. Kidder.   *Music by* Wm. B. Bradbury.

1. For many years we've waited To
   And now that day approaches, The

hail the day of peace, When our land should be united, And war and strife should cease;
drums are beating fast, And all the boys are coming home, There's victory at last.

FULL CHORUS.

There's vic - to - ry   at last,   boys,   vic - to - ry   at last!   O'er

land and sea Our flag is free; We'll nail it to tho mast; Yes, we'll

nail it to tho mast, boys, Nail it to tho mast; For there's

vic - to - ry, vic - to - ry, vic - to - ry at last!

2 The heroes who have gained it,
    And lived to see the day,
We will meet with flying banners
    And honors on the way;
And all their sad privations
    Shall to the winds be cast,
For all the boys are coming home —
    There's victory at last.—CHORUS.

3 O happy wives and children,
    Light up your hearts and homes,
For see, with martial music,
    "The conquering hero comes,"
With flags and streamers flying,
    While drums are beating fast;
For all the boys are coming home —
    There's victory at last.—CHORUS.

Sung at Fort Sumter, April 14, 1865.

See page 42.

APPENDIX.

----◆----

From the Charleston Mercury of January 19, 1865.

(A month before the evacuation of the city.)

CHARLESTON A SARAGOSSA !

*   *   *   *   *   *   *   *

"The same tenacity and daring which has held Charleston and
the Savannah line for four years, can hold Charleston now, if brought
to bear upon the emergency. Too long we have been fighting here,
around these old walls, to yield them now without a struggle. We
say, unhesitatingly, to those in authority, there are brave men here,
who are prepared to make of Charleston a second Saragossa. We
use no fancy phrase. We mean the exact thing. We mean fight
the country inch by inch to her outside lines; and we mean, then,
fight it inch by inch to the foot of old St. Michael's walls. *   *   *
We want no Atlanta, no Savannah business here. *   *   * Let
Charleston be strictly a military camp. The opportunity is offered
— let the commanding general make a fight here that will ring round
the world. We will not fail him. There are men here to do it.
We have made names historic before. We can do it now. Let us
strip and enter the arena for life or for death. Will he stand by
us?"

From the Charleston Mercury of February 10, 1865.

(A week before the evacuation of the city.)

"Amidst the dark shadows that envelop the destinies of the Confederate States at the present moment, we think — we dream perhaps, perhaps we imagine — that we see a faint streak of light,

struggling up across the eastern horizon through the darkness of the night. Is it the early messenger of morn? or is it an aurora of the night? Yet we imagine we see a streak of dawn upon the horizon. A new Yankee Congress comes in on the fourth of March next. What sort of body is it? Wild lunatics. They come into power flushed with success, and are themselves the very dregs of radicalism. Every one of them are drunken mobocrats and bloody Puritans of the deepest dye. What will they not do and say? Can Lincoln control them? Can Seward control them? We think not. In their very violence and brutality lies our hope. Can Europe stand them six months? We think not. Must not Europe see that if they are successful in destroying us, that their own time is not far off when they will be swept from off this continent? Will not this coming Yankee Congress force all the world either to cower before them, or check them by upholding us? We think it must. This is a streak of dawn that we imagine we see. Perhaps we are only nodding — and only dream. Still we fancy the thing. Let us stand to our arms, and watch for the morning."

The morning dawns at length.

From the Charleston Mercury, February 11, 1865.

(The last edition published in the city.)

To our Readers.

" The progress of military events, which has occasioned so much public and private inconvenience and suffering, has not spared the newspaper interest. The interruption of railroad communication between Charleston and the interior, produces a state of affairs which compels us, *temporarily*, to transfer the publication office of the *Mercury* elsewhere ; and to-day's paper will be our last issue, for the present, in the city of Charleston." (The editor then moved his establishment to Cheraw, S. C., directly in the line of General Sherman's advance.)

www.ingramcontent.com/pod-product-compliance
Lightning Source LLC
Chambersburg PA
CBHW030021030726
47499CB00008B/3063